FISHING: TIPS & TECHNIQUES™

WALLEYE FISHING

JUDY MONROE PETERSON

rosen publishing's rosen central
New York

To the DHP family, who love eating walleyes

Published in 2014 by The Rosen Publishing Group, Inc.
29 East 21st Street, New York, NY 10010

First Edition

Library of Congress Cataloging-in-Publication Data

Peterson, Judy Monroe.
Walleye fishing/Judy Monroe Peterson.—First edition.
pages cm—(Fishing: tips & techniques)
Includes bibliographical references and index.
ISBN 978-1-4488-9491-8 (library binding)—ISBN 978-1-4488-9510-6 (pbk.)—
ISBN 978-1-4488-9511-3 (6-pack)
1. Walleye fishing—Juvenile literature. I. Title.
SH691.W3P48 2014
799.17'75—dc23

2012047201

Manufactured in the United States of America

CPSIA Compliance Information: Batch #S13YA: For further information, contact Rosen Publishing, New York, New York, at 1-800-237-9932.

CONTENTS

INTRODUCTION

Walleyes are a prized freshwater sportfish and are found in the northern United States and Canada. Many southern states have stocked walleyes in selected waters. In numerous parts of North America, people can go fishing for walleyes on lakes and rivers during the spring, summer, and fall. Some people winter fish by cutting a hole through the ice on frozen lakes and dropping a line and hook. Walleyes readily take live bait or artificial lures and put up a strong, exciting battle when hooked, causing rods to bend sharply. They also present challenges to anglers because these fish travel in schools and move often in search of good food and water conditions. A walleye is excellent table fare because it is sweet and delicious. Successful fishers must study walleye habits and their living environment or they will probably go home empty-handed. The more skillful anglers become at locating walleyes, the more likely they are at catching them.

A wide variety of tackle and bait are available, as are numerous places to fish for walleyes. They can be fished with simple rods and reels along riverbanks or lakes. Some people fish in small-to-medium lakes from boats of various sizes, while others use

Anglers of all ages enjoy the excitement of catching walleyes. These fish are strong fighters, pulling hard and thrashing once they are hooked. Catching and eating a walleye is a memory that is long treasured.

sophisticated fishing boats on good-sized lakes. These big boats are built for windy weather conditions and big bodies of water with high waves. People can catch walleyes in rivers or lakes near their homes. Others go to fly-in resorts or cabins in remote parts of the United States as well as Canada. Once at the fly-in resort, they travel by boat to reach remote walleye schools.

Catching walleyes provides a good reason for people to get outdoors and have fun alone or with friends and family. Anglers can enjoy nature while fishing for walleyes, being careful to take safety precautions near and on the water. Many people find the most satisfying aspect of walleye fishing is eating the delicious, low-fat meat.

Because of walleye fishing's popularity as a freshwater sport and the fish's tasty meat, walleyes have been introduced into many lakes across North America. They have a close relative species called sauger. Adult saugers are smaller than walleyes, but usually are counted into legal walleye catch limits.

State and provincial fishing laws regulate the seasons of the year for walleye fishing. People are required to buy a fishing license to fish in designated walleye water or possess walleyes. Fishers need to know and follow the laws that are posted for the state or province in which they fish.

In many places across the United States, the natural environment of walleyes and other types of fish is endangered because of erosion and pollution. As a result, some fish populations are decreasing. Local citizens, state natural resource agencies, and the federal government are working together to improve walleye populations for anglers and for all who enjoy a great-tasting walleye meal.

CHAPTER 1

Basic Knowledge and Safety

The fishing environment requires care and preparation to master nature's laws. Staying safe on or near the water is an important priority for every person, as is respect for fish and the environment. Another essential aspect of fishing is being responsible to other people and property while catching fish. Basic courtesy goes a long way in making fishing trips fun for anglers and others who may be nearby, such as more fishers, swimmers, boaters, and hunters.

Preparing for a Safe Fishing Trip

Bringing the correct gear and other essential items for a fishing trip can contribute to angling success. Fishers should include sunblock to decrease the chance of developing serious sunburns from light reflecting off the surface of the water. They could also cover up

exposed skin with clothing. A hat with a large brim helps shield the skin and eyes from the sun. Wearing polarized sunglasses also protects the eyes and allows anglers to see below the surface of the water. Stinging and biting insects, such as gnats, black flies, mosquitoes, bees, and ticks, can make anglers miserable. Applying insect repellent before going near water is one way for anglers to keep these pests away.

Most people return from their fishing trip without having an accident. However, people might need to know how to treat minor injuries,

This father and son proudly hold their walleye trophies. An important piece of safety equipment is polarized sunglasses, which protect the eyes from bright sunlight that reflects off the water. They also shield them from hooks carelessly cast by nearby anglers.

such as getting a sharp hook out of a hand or face. Quick treatment of wounds reduces the chance of the injuries becoming infected, causing the fishing trip to end abruptly. To be prepared, people should bring a basic first-aid kit while on their outing and know how to use the items in the kit. Immediate medical attention is crucial if a serious injury occurs, such as a hook that is deep in the hand or face.

Wise anglers pay attention to the weather forecast before they go fishing on either riverbanks or a boat. While fishing, they should regularly scan the sky for changing weather conditions, such as sudden rain or a storm. People may see large gray clouds forming, hear thunder, or feel a cool wind before a storm rushes in. Another way to listen for changing weather is by using a radio or an application (app) on a smartphone.

By checking the weather before a fishing trip, anglers can wear the appropriate garb. They can bring a light rain jacket to keep from getting chilled. People should also dress in layers of comfortable clothes. Wearing a rain suit or waterproof clothing as the top layer and rubber boots will keep anglers dry and warm.

If a storm with lightning and thunder occurs, anglers on boats need to get to the shore immediately. Anyone on land should stay away from tall trees and other high objects and lay the fishing rod down or hold it parallel to the ground. Lightning is more likely to strike high objects.

Water Safety

A personal flotation device (PFD) is the most valuable safety equipment for all anglers. PFDs are also called life jackets or life vests. Many states and provinces have laws that require all people, while on the water, to wear U.S. Coast Guard–approved flotation gear. Even if this is not the law, anglers should wear a PFD when they are fishing in a boat or on riverbanks. These inflatable life jackets help people stay afloat and keep their head above water if they fall out of the boat.

When fishing from a boat, anglers need to learn boat control to safely and consistently catch walleyes. It is an important skill because many boats might be located in the same area when walleyes are being caught. Walleyes form tight schools, sometimes no larger than 3 feet (0.9 meter) across. The driver of the boat needs to pay strict attention to the location of other boats while trolling in a congested area. Drivers should slowly troll backward to give full attention to nearby anglers and boats. All people on a boat must watch for rocks, submerged trees, and sandbars that could snag the boat's motor. They should also keep an eye out for any litter and avoid it because it could entangle the boat motor or fishing equipment.

Sometimes boaters experience problems while fishing and need to get help. Wise fishers equip their boat with a signaling flag. This bright-orange flag provides a signal for help and is mandatory for use on some lakes. Anglers should also stock the boat with safety flares.

People can also go fishing for walleyes from riverbanks and docks. To avoid slipping and falling, anglers need to walk cautiously when they are around water. They should also take one careful step at a time along shorelines. These areas can be slick,

During spawning, walleyes swim in concentrated schools in shallow water. This behavior attracts anglers who tend to cluster on shorelines or in boats. Good sportsmanship is essential to protect the safety of all.

causing people to lose their footing. When preparing to fish from a dock, anglers should check that it's solid and secure. They need to look for sharp drop-offs and areas of strong undercurrent before wading into water. Fishers can wear rubber boots or tennis shoes to protect their feet from sharp stones or broken glass.

Using Equipment Safely

By carefully using their fishing equipment, anglers can avoid accidents. People should know where the rod tip is at all times and should not point it near others. When they're walking, anglers need to be sure that the hook is attached to a guide and the rod is pointed toward the sky. Another essential rule is always to look behind whenever casting.

The National Weather Service

A fishing trip may begin as a pleasant day for outdoor enthusiasts, but sudden rain or storms could surprise them. A reliable source of local weather warnings, watches, and forecasts is the National Oceanic and Atmospheric Administration (NOAA). This federal agency broadcasts local weather information from the nearest National Weather Service office, at any time or place. The weather alerts cover all states and are available by Internet (http://www.weather.gov), radio, smartphones, and other mobile devices.

Overhead casts are safer than side casts, which are more likely to hook someone. An overhead cast can also keep anglers from tangling their fishing line with someone else's line.

Anglers could get hand cuts or punctures if they are careless when handling fish. The walleye's teeth, grill covers, and dorsal fins are extremely sharp. To avoid injury, people need to handle the fish firmly or use a soft net to prevent it from flopping around in the water or boat. They should grip a walleye around the back of the head and above the gills.

Hooks are sharp and require attention when baiting them and removing them from a fish's mouth. A caught fish wiggles and flops around. If anglers grab a fish where it is hooked, they could get a hook into their hand or face. Experts recommend using needle-nosed pliers to remove a hook, working as carefully and quickly as possible.

Regulations

Every angler is responsible for maintaining and improving the sport of walleye fishing and fish habitats. People must follow the comprehensive fishing laws that most states have in place. Before going fishing, anglers need to know the regulations for the state or province, such as limits, legal hours, seasons for fishing walleyes, and purchasing a license. The license describes the number and size of walleyes that can be caught, and which lures, hooks, and baits can be used. In some states, people can buy a voluntary walleye stamp wherever fishing licenses are sold and online. The license and stamp purchases help sustain and improve walleye fishing, including fish stocking programs.

Mandatory catch and release of walleyes is the law in some areas. Even if they are not required to do so, anglers can release large adult walleyes. These fish are then left to reproduce, creating a new generation of walleyes that can be enjoyed by beginning and experienced fishers.

Fishery biologists research walleye populations and apply scientific principles to enhance future fishing opportunities. Mature, spawning fish are protected with catch-and-release regulations in many walleye habitats such as the one pictured here.

Anglers should not fish in areas where it is prohibited by federal or state law. They require the permission of the landowner to fish from private land. Otherwise, they're trespassing, which is illegal.

Sportsmanship

Good sportsmanship requires that a person follow the laws even when no one is looking or when the chance of being stopped by a game warden is low. It also includes being courteous to other people who are using a stream or lake for boating, swimming, and fishing.

When anglers find schools of walleyes, there may be many other people attracted to the same spot. Competing fishers need to give one another adequate space. For example, lines of people may be standing very close to one another, all casting from the shoreline of a river in which spawning walleyes are present. Anglers want to be careful to properly cast their hooks without injuring people next to or behind them. When walleyes are concentrated in lakes, the anglers' boats may become compacted into a small area. Fishers want to be sure that their boat's propeller is not cutting the lines of nearby anglers.

Sportsmanship extends to how people treat their living fish after the catch. If handled without touching the gills, walleyes can be caught, unhooked, and released. The number of walleyes living after being handled is very high if no serious bleeding has occurred and if the fish is immediately released back into the water. This type of catch-and-release fishing has contributed greatly to the walleye population in North America expanding, even when fishing pressure has increased.

CHAPTER 2

Getting Equipped

Anglers can go fishing for walleyes in different types of rivers and lakes. Based on the water that they will fish in, anglers can determine what equipment they will need. They require four basic tools to catch a walleye: a rod, a reel, fishing line, and hooks. Other important items are bobbers, weights, and sinkers or floats. One old, but successful, way to fish for walleyes is by using a cane pole, hook, and bobber.

People can find a huge assortment of other fishing equipment in sporting, bait, and other stores. Different fishing equipment and tackle is needed if they plan to fish from a shoreline or from a boat. Much of the gear common to walleye fishing in rivers and lakes includes rods, reels, lines, tackle, live bait hooks, bait boxes, pocket knives, clippers, pliers, and catching nets. Experienced anglers organize and store their tackle in a tackle box with a

As anglers gain experience, they usually move from using a hook, bobber, and worm to applying numerous tackle such as jigs and crankbaits. Valuable fishing tackle is best stored in a well-built tackle box.

handle and always take it on fishing trips. A notebook and pen can be kept in the tackle box by anglers and are handy for jotting down tackle that needs to be replaced or additional items to be purchased for the next outing.

Rods and Reels

Beginning anglers may want to use an inexpensive cane fishing pole, which is often made from a dried bamboo sapling. The beauty of a cane pole is that with only a little practice, fishers can place a baited hook in a very specific spot. This is especially important when placing a hook into open areas within a weed bed. A cane pole can be up to 10 feet (3 m) in length, with an attached line that is two-thirds of the pole's length. Anglers can slowly whip the tip of the pole overhead to provide precise direction for placement of the bait where walleyes may be feeding.

Anglers can also fish with a rod and reel. Rods are thin, strong poles that vary in length and thickness. Fiberglass or graphite rods are preferred because they are lightweight, flexible, and strong. To select a rod, fishers need to consider its length, weight, and action. The length is the longest measurement of an object, and the weight is the type of line that works best for the rod. Line comes in weights from one (lightest) to twelve (heaviest). Anglers use light line when fishing for small walleyes from the shoreline and heavy lines for large walleyes in big lakes.

Depending on the type of river or lake fished, walleye anglers usually prefer rods of longer length. These rods cast better because they provide additional energy in the line for greater distance and precision for placement of the hook. They also give anglers more control when fighting a forceful walleye and pick up slack line better before setting the hook. Action is how much a rod bends and rebounds when casting. After a walleye is caught, the longer rod held at a forty-five-degree angle forces the fish to use its energy faster by fighting the bowed rod. Beginning anglers may want to start with a medium-action rod when fishing for walleyes in either rivers or lakes.

A popular rod-and-reel combination for all-purpose walleye fishing is a 5.5- to 6-foot (1.7- to 1.8-m) spinning rod and matching open-face spinning reel. Closed-face spinning reels are also an excellent choice for beginning anglers because they are very easy to use. Advanced fishers often carry several rod-and-reel outfits because they try different techniques during a day of walleye fishing. For casting with small lures and live bait, a 5- to 5.5-foot (1.5- to 1.7-m), light-power, fast-action

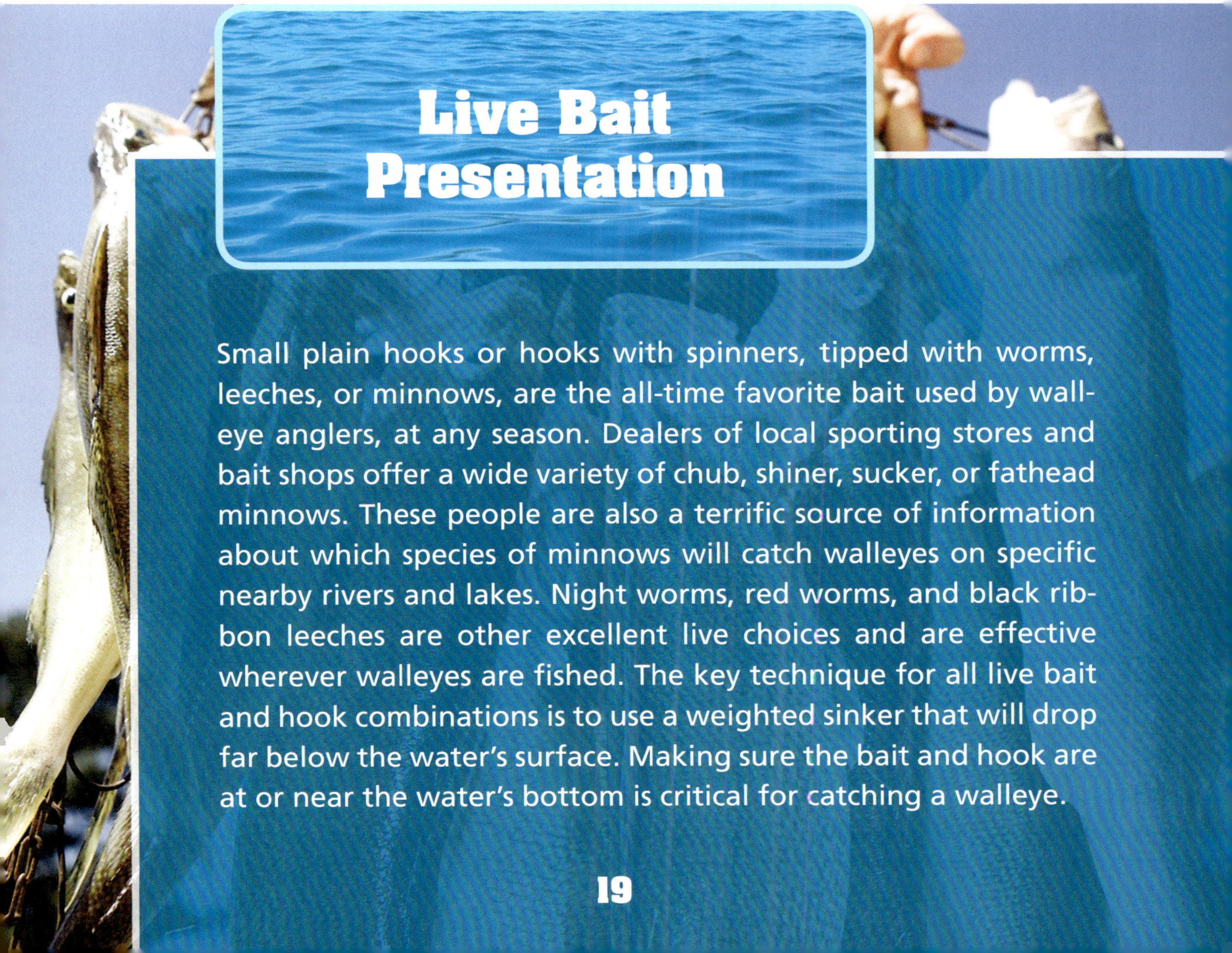

Live Bait Presentation

Small plain hooks or hooks with spinners, tipped with worms, leeches, or minnows, are the all-time favorite bait used by walleye anglers, at any season. Dealers of local sporting stores and bait shops offer a wide variety of chub, shiner, sucker, or fathead minnows. These people are also a terrific source of information about which species of minnows will catch walleyes on specific nearby rivers and lakes. Night worms, red worms, and black ribbon leeches are other excellent live choices and are effective wherever walleyes are fished. The key technique for all live bait and hook combinations is to use a weighted sinker that will drop far below the water's surface. Making sure the bait and hook are at or near the water's bottom is critical for catching a walleye.

spinning rod is a good choice. Casting and trolling in deep streams and lakes calls for a 5.5- to 6-foot (1.7- to 1.8-m) medium-power, fast-action, bait-casting rod.

Spinning outfits are great for both large river and lake fishing, and spin-casting rigs are also effective. In spin-cast equipment, the line spool is sometimes covered in housing that is at the top of the reel. With closed-faced rods, anglers cast the line outward by simply depressing the trigger and then releasing as the rod brings the lure forward. The line spins off the end of a spool and passes out through a hole in the reel cover. Monofilament line in the 6- to -15-pound (2.7- to -6.8-kilogram) class usually does not tangle inside the cover.

Jigs and Crankbaits

Anglers can find a bewildering array of artificial baits commonly used for walleye fishing in large sporting goods stores or on the Internet. Lures are extremely effective when tipped with live minnows, worms, or leeches. They can often be used without tipping them with live bait, which can save anglers some money. All fishers should have lures in their tackle box, readily available for action.

Jigs are hooks with a molded body of lead, lead substitute, or molded foam plastic that either sinks to the bottom of the water or remains floating on the surface. The head's shape makes the bait move through the water with different movements. Jigs are available in weights between 1/16 to 1 ounce (1.8 to 23.3 grams). Anglers use the heavy varieties to sink the bait into fast-moving river waters. Walleyes tend to live on or near the water's bottom, and jigs bring the bait directly to the fish's location.

Floating jigs with bodies of foam allow the bait to float above the water's bottom when a sinker is attached to the line at a distance equal

Jigs, tipped with live bait or artificial latex worms, are favorite walleye-catching tackle. Jigs with a heavy molded body quickly sink to the water's bottom where hungry walleye are lurking.

to where the angler wants the bait presented. They can be used for trolling, casting, or by jigging straight up and down off the side of a boat. Jigs of all varieties tipped with a minnow are a favorite combination for winter fishing through holes in the ice.

Crankbaits are artificial lures made of wood, plastic, or foam that usually have attached treble hooks. They are effective for casting or trolling. Experienced anglers know that crankbaits are an extremely effective way to catch walleyes feeding in shallow water. These artificial lures are the best choice when casting during sunset, sunrise, and nighttime. It is important for fishers to have several different styles

Instant Access to Walleye Lake Maps

In many states, the department of natural resources offers hydrological maps of walleye lakes on their Web site. Anglers with smartphones, tablets, or similar electronic devices can instantly access these maps while they are fishing. They can then determine exactly where a lake bottom feature is located that may hold a school of hungry walleyes. For example, the Minnesota Department of Natural Resources provides excellent hydrological maps of the state's fishing lakes at http://www.dnr.state.mn.us/lakefind/index.html. Maine posts its lake survey maps at http://www.maine.gov/ifw/fishing/lakesurvey_maps/index.htm.

in the tackle box because crankbaits are made to retrieve walleyes at different depths.

Other Useful Tools

Many outdoor enthusiasts, including walleye anglers, carry a smartphone or a small Global Positioning System (GPS) unit, which provides instant access to global position locations with latitude and longitude coordinates. The GPS allows people to travel around large lakes or walk shorelines and return at their starting point. More important, anglers can use these tools to keep track of where walleyes were biting and return to those exact spots.

Smartphones and many similar small electronic devices contain a digital camera. With this camera, anglers can take fishing action photographs and immediately send them to family and friends over the

Internet. Many anglers carry waterproof digital cameras to document their great fish catches, especially when the catch will be released.

Boats

As anglers become advanced in the techniques of walleye fishing, they usually begin to fish from boats. Shoreline fishing is productive, but it

Fishing walleyes from small boats allows anglers to access sunken islands and sandbars that are far offshore. Anglers often troll backward to position the boat directly over a feeding school of walleye.

doesn't allow full access to walleye habitat. Boats used by anglers are found in a wide range of styles, sizes, and prices. Canoes and flatboats propelled by paddles and oars are also common for fishing. A popular canoe that provides more room and stability is called a sportsboat. They are made of aluminum and have a square stern for mounting a 2- to 10-foot (0.6- to 3-m) outboard motor. Depending on the size of a lake destination, boats of 16- to 22-feet (4.9- to 6.7-m) in length are the preferred choice of walleye fishers.

Boats are used to troll at slow speeds over walleye habitat. To accomplish this quietly, many boaters attach a strong electric-powered motor. Outboard motors in the five to twenty horsepower range run so quietly that anglers often use them to move the boat backward over or near the intended walleye habitat.

CHAPTER 3

UNDERSTANDING WALLEYES

Walleyes are native to North America from the Rocky Mountains to the Appalachian Mountains, and from Canada to Texas. They have also been introduced to other states. However, anglers in the South may not have as many places to fish as those in the North because walleyes prefer cool water. Because of the fish's popularity with anglers and because it's a delicious food, both Minnesota and South Dakota have declared the walleye as their state fish.

Walleye Basics

People named the walleye for its large, glossy white eyes or "walleyed" stare, which is caused by a reflective layer in the fish's eye. Other names for this fish include walleyed pike, pike perch, pickerel, yellow pickerel, yellow walleye, marble eye, and

Sauger *(top)* and walleyes look similar. Anglers look for the white spot on the lower tail to quickly identify a walleye. Good fishers identify the species of fish they catch to follow fishing regulations.

glass eye. In Canada, walleyes are also known as jackfish or doré. The walleye is the largest member of the perch family and is not related to the northern pike.

To identify a walleye, anglers need to look for a handsome fish with a slender body, a white belly, and two large fins with sharp spines. A dark mark is at the rear of the fin. The tail is slightly forked, with a prominent white area on the lower lobe. Walleyes can be a dark olive brown to yellowish gold with sides that are often marked with brassy flecks or stripes along the side. In clear rivers and lakes, they often have a golden hue, but they are usually grayish in very muddy water. The fast-swimming walleye has needlelike, sharp teeth.

The length and weight of walleyes vary greatly, depending on their age and habitat. Most walleyes live ten years or less, although they can survive twenty years or more. In the Midwest and Canada, it takes about six years for a walleye to reach 2 pounds (0.9 kg) and a length of 17 inches (42.2 centimeters).

Beginning anglers may confuse walleyes, saugers, and saugeyes because they look alike, often live in the same rivers and lakes, and can be fished using similar methods. In addition, all three are very tasty. Fishers, though, can look for distinct differences between them. Saugers are a close cousin of walleyes and are found all over the United States. They are about 18 inches (45.7 cm) in length and usually weigh less than 3 pounds (1.4 kg). A walleye and sauger may spawn together, and the result is a saugeye, which is similar in appearance to its parents. The fast-growing saugeye is between 13 and 16 inches (33.0 and 40.6 cm) in length and weighs an average of 1 pound (0.4 kg). Like a sauger, an adult saugeye is usually counted into legal walleye catch limits.

Compared to a walleye, the smaller and slimmer sauger has several rows of distinct black spots on the dorsal fin and a dark spot at the bottom of the pectoral fins. The overall body color is blackish or grayish. The forked tail of the sauger has a pale streak on the bottom edge, but it does not have the prominent white spot found on a walleye. The best way to identify the saugeye is by the distinct, long dark bars on the sides. The lower part of the tail and anal fins are tipped in white.

Senses and Behavior

In addition to being able to identify walleyes, successful fishers need to understand the amazing senses that influence their behavior. By studying the annual life cycle of a walleye, anglers can predict where the

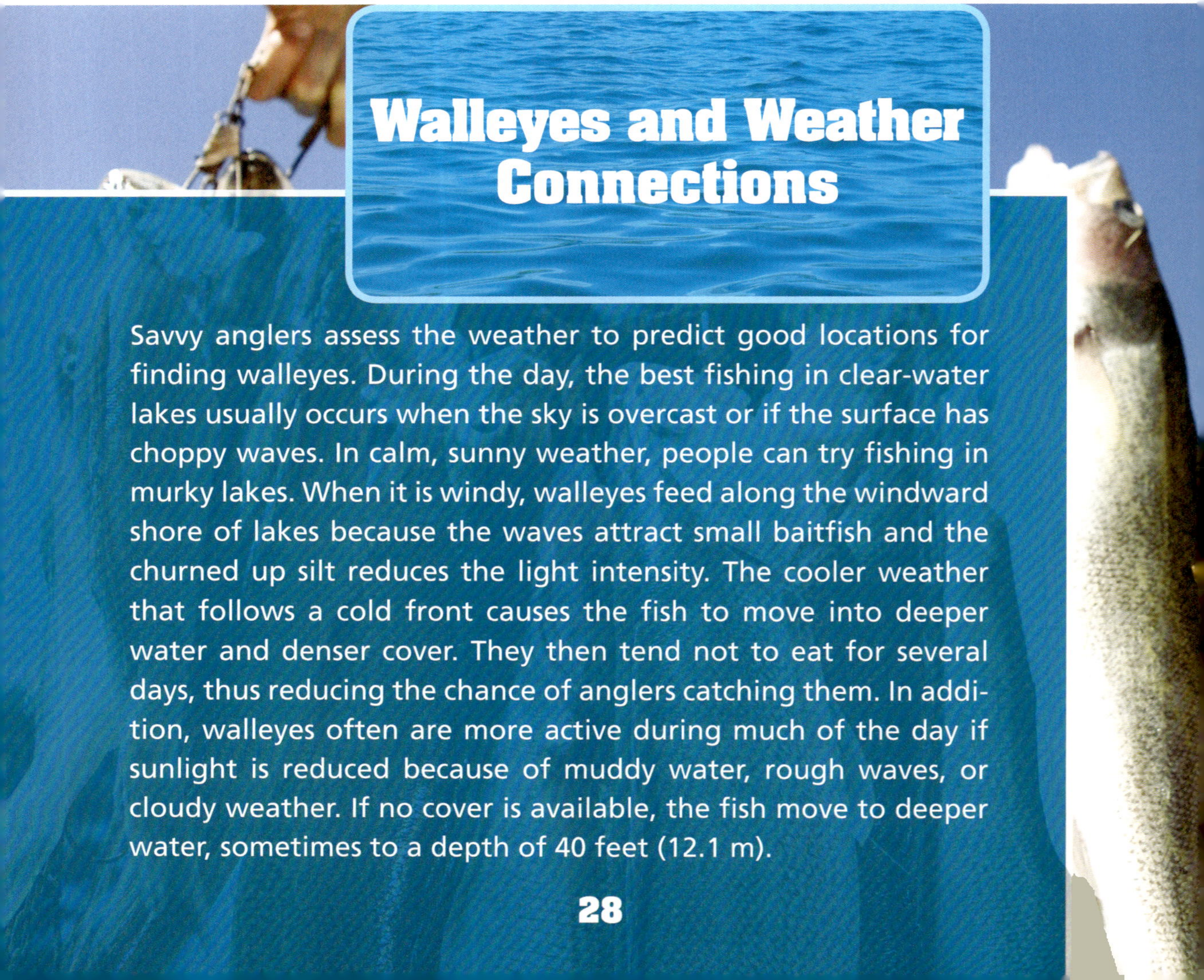

Walleyes and Weather Connections

Savvy anglers assess the weather to predict good locations for finding walleyes. During the day, the best fishing in clear-water lakes usually occurs when the sky is overcast or if the surface has choppy waves. In calm, sunny weather, people can try fishing in murky lakes. When it is windy, walleyes feed along the windward shore of lakes because the waves attract small baitfish and the churned up silt reduces the light intensity. The cooler weather that follows a cold front causes the fish to move into deeper water and denser cover. They then tend not to eat for several days, thus reducing the chance of anglers catching them. In addition, walleyes often are more active during much of the day if sunlight is reduced because of muddy water, rough waves, or cloudy weather. If no cover is available, the fish move to deeper water, sometimes to a depth of 40 feet (12.1 m).

fish will be concentrated in a specific area because of spawning. Two important characteristics of walleyes greatly influence their behavior: low-light vision and lateral-line sense. Walleyes are predators, and in dim light, they can see much better than their prey, such as small yellow perch. This unique hunting advantage comes from the highly reflective layer in a walleye's eye. It provides good light conditions for walleyes to feed because their prey fish have limited vision but remain active.

The lateral-line system helps a walleye pinpoint the location and travel direction of schools of baitfish, such as small perch. These highly sensitive nerve endings on each side of the body can detect tiny vibrations in the water. Anglers can use the fish's lateral line sense to their advantage because a walleye can locate an artificial lure in murky or deep water.

Walleyes don't like noise when they're in shallow water. To escape loud sounds, they move to deeper water or dense cover. Experts recommend quietly anchoring and casting to the walleye when fishing in a boat where the water is less than 10 feet (3 m) deep. They also advise against trolling through shallow water.

Eating Habits

Like many other fish, walleyes often school up. This behavior makes them easier for anglers to catch—if they can find them. Sometimes fishers have difficulty locating a school because these efficient and quick predators constantly move in search of food and are usually in different spots from day to day. They eat often and feed throughout the year on different prey.

Their main diet is small fish, such as perch, suckers, alewives, smelt, shad, shiners, cisco, sculpin, minnows, darters, and even small walleyes. They enjoy mollusks such as crayfish and meaty animals like frogs, worms, and leeches. Walleyes will also eat aquatic insects, such as lake

Walleyes move into shallow water and feed in schools as twilight and darkness descend. Many walleyes have been caught at sunset by casting floating crankbaits from shoreline rocks, beaches, and docks.

flies or mayflies, during a large hatch in early spring.

Walleyes tend to feed most often in the morning, evening, and night, which can be successful times to go fishing. However, experienced anglers know that water color and turbidity (muddiness) play a large role in the feeding habits of this fish. Many walleye lakes have dark water, which can make for good daytime fishing.

Habitat

Anglers can find walleyes in large, deep, freshwater rivers or lakes that are greater than 50 to 100 acres (0.2 sq km). They thrive in cool water, from 65 to 75 degrees Fahrenheit (18.3 to 23.9 degrees Celsius), even living under the cover of ice in the winter. They prefer a water bottom of rock, gravel, or sand. Sometimes walleyes search for bottom terrain that is very different from their surroundings. For example, if a bottom is sand, people can try fishing near rocky points and loose piles of rock. However, anglers may want to find sandy and weedy areas if the lake bottom is rocky.

Beginners may have the best chance of catching walleyes if they choose large rivers and lakes with moderate amounts of plant cover, which allows the fish to feed and escape the sun's rays on clear days. Walleyes are known as "structure fish" because they hide under the cover of sunken islands, rocky piles and points, submerged trees, reef systems, and brush piles. Other favorite structures are sandbars and rock bars. Anglers can also find walleyes in shallow areas that have

In the spring, anglers can catch hungry walleye's on small streams and rivers. Shoreline fishing is inexpensive, requiring only a casting rod and some essential tackle.

deep weed edges and beds. Except for winter, walleyes can live in weedy areas that are less than 12 feet (3.6 m) of water.

Walleyes prefer large structures. If structures are small, baitfish often swim to other areas when chased by predators. However, small fish usually remain on and around large structures even if walleyes are hunting them. Structures that have irregular surfaces or edges attract walleyes because their prey is likely to feed or hide there.

Depending on the season, walleyes move to different structures. In the spring, they spawn in shallow water and often stay around the structures along the sand, rock, or gravel shoreline. Early summer may still be a good time to catch walleyes along shorelines with sharp drops of rock or gravel. However, during the summer, they move to structure in deeper, cooler water as the surface of the river or lake becomes warmer. Then fishers can find them near sunken islands, sandbars, and deep shoreline points. Walleyes are likely found on reef and large lake points in and around deep water in the fall. People can fish for walleyes through the ice that forms on lakes and reservoirs in the winter. Walleyes actively feed on live bait hooks throughout the winter. Good places to look for the fish in cold winter months are on lake bottoms that have boulder piles or larger reefs.

CHAPTER 4

Taking Care of the Catch

Anglers must know the local license requirements for catching walleyes, including how many and the size that can be kept and which tackle, live bait, and lure can be used. One regulation found in many areas of the United States is mandatory catch and release of live walleyes. Even if not required, many people release adult walleyes that they catch. These large walleyes can then reproduce, which helps maintain a strong fish population for future anglers to enjoy.

Fishers often keep their legal walleyes for eating. A walleye is a nutritional, delicious meal any time of the year, but some walleyes may be tainted from pollution. People should follow the pollution postings for a particular river or lake to make sure it is safe to eat the fish.

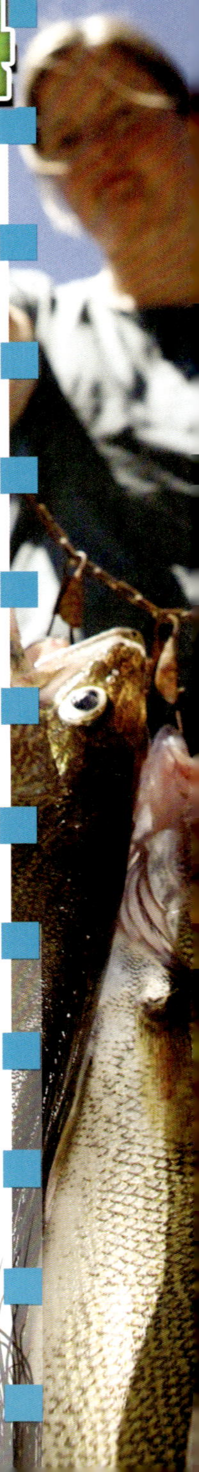

Fishing Regulations

Regulations of freshwater game fish such as walleyes promote healthy fish populations, increasing the chance of people making a catch. Although fishing laws apply throughout a state, the laws may change each year based on studies regularly conducted by fishery biologists. These scientists study fish in rivers and lakes to maintain or restore their habitats.

Anglers could catch too many fish because they have many technological advantages. The Internet and many other resources provide a wealth of information about the habits and habitats of walleyes and can instantly alert fishers to areas where fish are concentrated. GPS units, underwater cameras, and depth finders make it possible for anglers to catch many fish during a trip.

Fishery biologists handle and study walleyes, their habitat, and environment. With heavy fishing pressure on walleye populations, it is essential that present populations be protected from overfishing.

As a result, most states have regulations to keep walleye populations healthy. Laws specify the fishing methods that can be used. Many rivers and lakes have daily catch limits on popular fish so that people cannot keep too many fish. Regulations specify the dates for the fishing seasons. In many states, walleyes must reach a minimum size limit before they can be kept to help protect the fish until they are spawning size.

Before a fishing trip, people need to know a state's fishing regulations. They can find these rules on a state's Web site, state department of natural resources Web site, or in booklets at sporting goods stores. In addition, the state department of natural resources often posts this information at public access sites and piers.

Catch and Release

Using proper handling techniques improves the chance of survival of released fish. Anglers should try to keep a walleye in water or near the surface while gently removing a hook and handle it as little as possible. If the gills are damaged, the fish may soon die because it cannot take in enough water and oxygen. Cutting the line is recommended if the hook is deep in the fish. Some walleyes will survive with hooks left in them.

Anglers may be able to remove the hook from a fish in water by pulling on the line and then working the hook out of the walleye's mouth.

This walleye is being released in northern Minnesota. Anglers need to wet their hands, net, towel, or gloves before touching a catch-and-release walleye. Without the water, the hands, net, and other objects remove the fish's protective slime coating and scales.

Sometimes, though, a hook may get caught on a hand or finger. Many fishers use barbless hooks or flatten the barbs on a standard hook with pliers. Barbless hooks are easy to remove from the fish's mouth or an angler's finger.

If people need to take the fish out of the water for hook removal, they should avoid injuring the walleye's protective slime layer. This layer helps keep fish from developing infections. Fishers also should not touch the fish with dry hands or place them on rocks, sand, docks, or other dry surfaces. Instead, they can use wet hands, wet towels, or a soft rubber net to keep the walleye in water or to lift it out of the water, if necessary. A soft net helps reduce injuring the fish's protective slime layer.

Once a hook is free, anglers should make sure the walleye is in good condition before releasing it. To do this, they gently place the fish in the water. If the fish can stay upright or swim, it can be released. A fish that is not moving needs to be revived by holding it upright and gently moving it upstream. Fresh water containing oxygen can now flow through the gills. When the walleye begins to move, anglers can then release it and allow the fish to swim away.

Keeping a Walleye Safe for Eating

Once the excitement of catching a walleye is enjoyed, people need to keep it safe for delicious eating. The most important guide is to keep the fish as fresh as possible by being sure it is cold at all times. All fish can quickly spoil if proper care is not taken while fishing.

Using a stringer in the water is one way to hold fish. Live wells, available on many larger fishing boats, are another short-term storage option. Fishers should place the catch in the live well immediately, making sure that fresh water is continually pumped in.

Ice fishing on frozen lakes only requires a simple hook and live bait dropped near the bottom of the water. Anglers also jig with a minnow.

Keeping fish on ice prevents it from spoiling or getting a fishy taste. Anglers can either ice live fish after catching them or clean them immediately and then place them on ice. People can bring a cooler filled with ice or put ice into a live well to store their catch.

Preparing and Cooking Walleyes

To prepare a walleye for cooking, anglers need to learn how to use a sharp, long knife to cut the fish into two strips of meat. These strips, one from each side of the belly, are called fillets. With a little practice, people can quickly and easily produce tasty fillets and keep wasted meat to a minimum.

Anglers use a variety of methods to fillet a walleye. One way is to lay the fish on its side and make a cut behind the pectoral fin straight down the backbone. Next, they make a deep vertical cut just below the gills, from the top of the fish to the bottom. Then they cut over the backbone and down the ribs and through the belly flap. This technique releases a fillet. A similar cut on the other side produces a second fillet. It is important to remove and discard the fat along the back, belly, and sides of fish because pollutants are concentrated in the fish's fat. Finally, the skeleton and offal are wrapped in newspaper and discarded in the trash, and the fillets are rinsed in cold water. A walleye is best cooked right away, or it can be placed in a plastic storage bag and refrigerated for one or two days. Freezing the fillets in water is necessary for longer storage.

Walleyes are greatly prized for home and restaurant meals because of their superb sweet, delicate flavor. The meat is lean, nutritious, and flaky white when cooked. People enjoy fried fish fillets for a shore lunch, but this fish is adaptable to many cooking methods, including baking, grilling, broiling, microwaving, poaching, sautéing, pan frying, and deep frying. Walleye chowder or stews are popular. When fully cooked, a walleye turns opaque (milky) and flakes easily.

Preserving the Memory

With the popularity of catch-and-release fishing, photography is an important way to remember a great catch or trip. People can stow a camera in the tackle box or on the boat to document any memorable fish or moments of the trip. Fishers need to take photos right away, while the fish is held in water or taken out of water. This helps keep the fish alive when released. To make the photos look real and

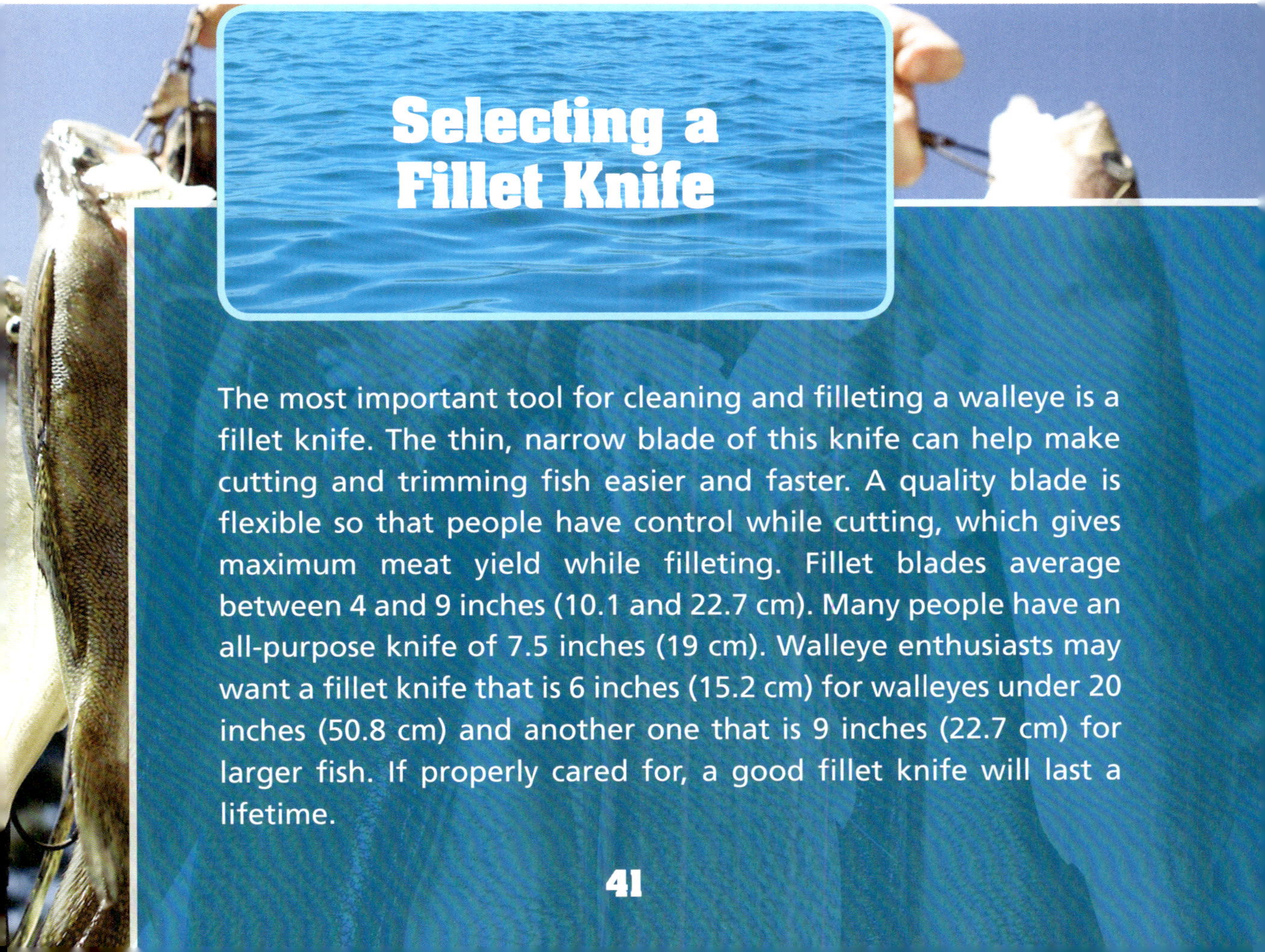

Selecting a Fillet Knife

The most important tool for cleaning and filleting a walleye is a fillet knife. The thin, narrow blade of this knife can help make cutting and trimming fish easier and faster. A quality blade is flexible so that people have control while cutting, which gives maximum meat yield while filleting. Fillet blades average between 4 and 9 inches (10.1 and 22.7 cm). Many people have an all-purpose knife of 7.5 inches (19 cm). Walleye enthusiasts may want a fillet knife that is 6 inches (15.2 cm) for walleyes under 20 inches (50.8 cm) and another one that is 9 inches (22.7 cm) for larger fish. If properly cared for, a good fillet knife will last a lifetime.

attractive, they should be taken during regular fish-handling activities and in natural lighting early or late in the day.

Some people have a taxidermist make a fish reproduction, which is identical to the one caught and released. These professionals make a plastic model of the walleye based on photos, its measurements, and position that anglers want. Once complete, anglers can proudly display the replica mount in their home or cabin. A taxidermist can also make a trophy mount from the actual walleye skin. This method requires careful preservation of the fish immediately after catching it. Today, many people are choosing plastic replica mounts instead of mounting the actual fish.

CHAPTER 5

MANAGING WALLEYE FISHING AND THE ENVIRONMENT

Many people think walleyes are the best-tasting freshwater fish. They are fished both recreationally and commercially for food. Fish markets and restaurants can charge high prices and attract customers for fresh walleye fillets because of great demand.

Human activity, such as overfishing, water pollution, and loss of natural habitats, can cause huge problems for fish. The federal government, states, and provinces work together to protect the water where fish live. In addition, anglers can help keep fish and their habitats clean and safe.

Walleyes and Tourism

Fishing is a growing hobby in North America,

Walleye fillets, deep-fried to a golden brown, produce a white, flaky, and delicious meal for anyone. Dining on walleye is a treat and makes fishing for this fish a compelling hobby.

and walleyes are greatly valued game fish. Nearby towns and cities can benefit financially from sport fishing and tourism. Each year, hundreds of millions of dollars are generated by fishing activities. Local communities prosper because anglers buy tackle, outdoor clothing, boats, motors, food, and gas.

Every state and provincial department of natural resources controls walleyes because they are a valuable fish population. Governments have successfully introduced walleyes into lakes and rivers to maintain and increase the fish population. These programs have stimulated and encouraged a strong growth in tourism across the Midwest and Canada.

Overfishing and Declining Fish Populations

Overfishing is the harvesting of too many fish, causing the population to drop to a dangerous level. Various commercial fish throughout the world are overfished. One example is the Atlantic menhaden, which is important in marine ecosystems from Maine to Florida. This tiny fish makes up a large part of the diet of striped bass, tuna, cod, dolphins, whales, eagles, and other predators. Each year, fishing crews haul in hundreds of millions of menhaden, which become pet food, fertilizer, feed for farm-raised fish and other farm animals, and dietary supplements for people.

The population of the Atlantic menhaden is now at a record-low level, and not enough fish are left to reproduce. As a result, the health and numbers of striped bass and other marine fish that eat menhaden are decreasing. In turn, this is impacting the commercial and sport fishing industries along the East Coast.

Caught mainly in state waters, menhaden are managed by the Atlantic States Marine Fisheries Commission (ASMFC), not by federal or individual state governments. The ASMFC has defined safe fishing targets for this fish, but they are not enforced.

Water Pollution and Climate Change

Water pollution can seriously harm fish. Pollution occurs when pollutants build up in water and contaminate it. Heavy metals like mercury and lead, silt, oils, animal waste, and other contaminants enter water directly or when attached to raindrops from mining, manufacturing, logging, and farming operations. Poisonous chemicals come from burning coal and the fuel used to run vehicles and airplanes. Large chemical and oil spills that flow into the water can kill fish fast. If a ship ruptures its oil tanks, enormous amounts of oil can spill into the sea or inland waters.

Other actions can cause major contamination of water. Until the 1970s, anglers nationwide went walleye fishing in the Saginaw River in Michigan. However, factories and city wastewater treatment plants had been dumping polychlorinated biphenyls (PCBs) into the river since the 1940s. PCBs, once widely used in paints, adhesives, and some electrical equipment, were banned by the federal government in 1979 because they can cause birth defects, cancer, liver damage, and nerve disorders in people, fish, and other animals. Since then, PCB levels in the river have dramatically decreased, especially after more than 340,000 cubic yards (260 million cubic meters) of polluted sediment was removed in 2000 and 2001. Today, the walleye population in Saginaw River has soared and once again draws anglers from across the country.

Normal quantities of nutrients are essential to aquatic animals and plants. They come from the air or from leaves or other living matter that falls into rivers and lakes. Water pollution can add too many of these otherwise necessary nutrients, causing an unnatural growth in the numbers of algae (plantlike organisms), plants, fish, and other animals. The fast-growing algae can form a green scum on the water that blocks the light needed by plants to produce oxygen. Without enough oxygen, walleyes and other living aquatic things die.

Walleyes and other fish are usually healthy to eat. However, they may contain contaminants such as mercury that could harm people's health. State departments of health offer safe eating guidelines

Pollutants often reside in streams, rivers, and lakes. The pollutants are found in walleyes that eat contaminated, smaller fish. Wise anglers always check local postings to make certain that the walleyes can be safely eaten.

for walleyes and different fish. State and provincial departments of natural resources also publish warnings about polluted waters and recommendations for eating fish. This information can be found in a free pamphlet or on the departments' Web sites.

Earth's climate is getting warmer, mostly because of human activity that creates increased amounts of greenhouse gases. Global warming is resulting in different weather patterns, higher sea levels, and earlier melting of snow and ice in the spring. These changes affect people, animals, and ecosystems in many ways. The food supplies, life cycles, and reproduction or spawning habits of animals may change, and some plants and animals will have trouble surviving. The warming of Earth has led to higher river and lake temperatures, which can make many lakes too warm for cold water fish such as walleyes. These fish may adapt to the changing conditions, move north, decrease in population, or vanish if the climate continues to warm.

Managing America's Water

In the United States, federal and state governments work to keep the nation's water and fish clean and safe. In 1972, the U.S. Congress passed the Federal Water Pollution Control Act, commonly known as the Clean Water Act. This law sets strict limits on the substances that industries can discharge into the U.S. waterways. The Environmental Protection Agency administers this law, which includes maintaining and restoring safe water and protecting fish habitats.

Another federal agency, the U.S. Fish and Wildlife Service, is dedicated to the management of fish, wildlife, and natural habitats. It is responsible for the National Fish Hatchery System, which operates seventy hatcheries in thirty-five states. This program restores declining fish populations resulting from drought, flood, overfishing, or

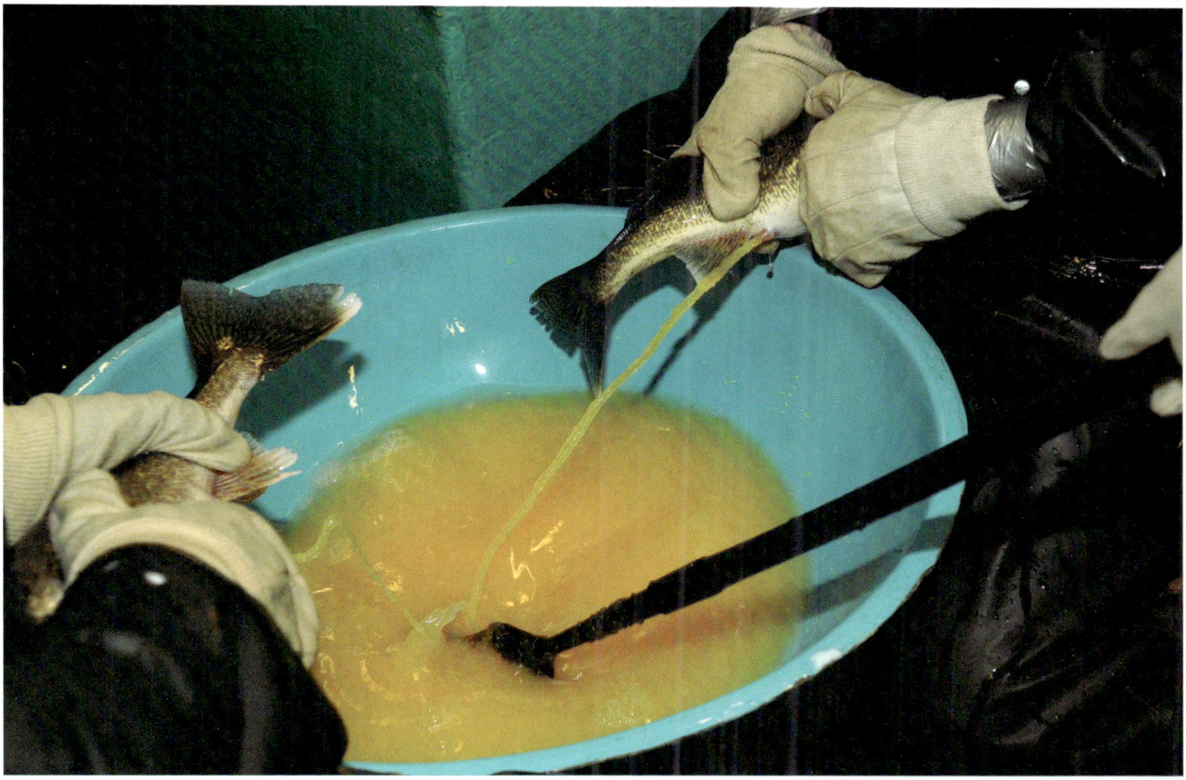

At this hatchery in upstate New York, workers created artificial walleye spawning by mixing the yellow eggs from an adult female with the sperm of an adult male. The fertilized walleye eggs are then raised in the hatchery and later released in the state's lakes to replenish stocks.

other events. The agency also protects and conserves fish and their habitats. The hatcheries artificially spawn fish eggs and then raise and release the fry (recently hatched small fish). Tens of millions of walleye fry are stocked for sport fishing each year.

All states and provinces have a department of natural resources that maintains, improves, and restores water, fish habitats, and walleye populations. To fish, anglers must purchase an annual fishing license. The money is used to fund the enforcement of laws and keep water clean and walleye populations healthy.

Working Together for Safe Water

Game fish in North America are an important resource, and anglers can help protect fish, wildlife, water, and forests. People can do this by fishing in approved areas that safeguard wildlife or vegetation. Fishers must use approved live bait and follow the seasons and limits on the number and size of fish that are caught and remain in possession. It is important that people properly dispose of used monofilament fishing line and other trash because fish, shore birds, and other animals might swallow hooks or become tangled in discarded fishing line and die. In many states, it is illegal to dump unused worms, minnows, leeches, or other bait into rivers and lakes. Excess bait can be disposed of in a trash can at the access point or boat landing or taken home for proper discarding.

Young people have many opportunities to become involved in local cleanup efforts of streams, rivers, and lakes. They can ask their

The Great Lakes Water Quality Agreement

In 1972, the Great Lakes Water Quality Agreement was signed into law by the United States and Canada. Together, the five Great Lakes contain 20 percent of the world's fresh surface water and 90 percent of the freshwater in the United States. The regulations, which were amended in 2012, protect the lakes from industrial discharge and runoff of poisonous substances from farming, aquatic invasive species, loss of animal habitat, and the effects of climate change.

teacher or school to adopt a stream and rid it of trash. Youth groups such as the Boy and Girl Scouts often work to keep a specific walleye stream or lake clean. After a flood, local governments may ask for young volunteers to clean stream and lake shorelines.

Preparing for More Walleye Fishing

Preparing for the next trip takes only a short time, but it helps ensure catching the wily walleye. The first step is to clean and inspect all rods, reels, tools, and tackle for damage. Fishers can make a list of tackle to replace and of other items necessary for the next trip. The exact locations of where walleyes were caught become critical for returning in the future. Savvy anglers keep a journal, carefully noting on maps or with latitude and longitude coordinates where great fishing was discovered.

Walleye anglers often join fishing clubs, read books and magazine articles, or find information on the Internet to learn how to become more skillful. States and even areas of certain states have fishing clubs, some specific to walleyes. Most often, these clubs will have a junior angler club within a parent club that is expressly for younger anglers. Social networking and online forums are popular for teaching and can connect anglers to other people who have similar interests in catching a walleye, North America's most valued fish.

GLOSSARY

angler A person who uses a hook and line to catch fish.
bait The food used to attract fish to hooks.
catch and release The return of a caught fish to the water.
conserve To protect and preserve nature.
crankbait An artificial lure that is retrieved by cranking the reel.
dorsal fin The fin found on the top of a fish's back.
fly-in resort A vacation or recreation destination where seaplanes are used to reach it.
gill The organ of fish that breathes water to obtain oxygen.
graphite A form of carbon.
habitat A place where a living thing is naturally found.
hatchery A place where scientists allow fish eggs to hatch.
invasive A plant or animal outside of its home range.
jig A kind of artificial bait that is jerked up and down through the water.
lure A nonfood object with hooks placed at the end of a fishing line to attract fish.
monofilament A very thin fishing line made from nylon.
offal The waste parts of a fish, such as the internal organs and head.
pollutant A harmful manmade substance found in natural environments.
predator An animal that hunts and feeds on other animals.
prey An animal hunted or caught for food.
sandbar A ridge of sand formed in a river or along a shore by the action of waves or currents.
sauger A close cousin of a walleye that is found all over the United States.
saugeye A species created in hatcheries by mating a walleye with a sauger.

school A group of fish.
season The days of the year when it is legal to fish.
spawning When male fish spread sperm onto female eggs.
species A group of animals with similar features that produce offspring.
spin-casting Fishing with a light rod and reel that has a device that guides the line around a stationary spool and that can be disengaged to let the line freely release when casting.
spinner A flashy blade that rotates rapidly on a lure.
tackle A general term for an angler's equipment.
tresspass To unlawfully enter a person's property.
troll To fish by trailing a baited hook or lure through the water from a moving boat.

For More Information

American Sportfishing Association
225 Reinekers Lane, Suite 420
Alexandria, VA 22314
(703) 519-9691
Web site: http://www.asafishing.org
The American Sportfishing Association provides information about angling and the sportsfishing business.

Association of Fish and Wildlife Agencies
444 North Capitol Street NW, Suite 725
Washington, DC 20001
(202) 624-7890
Web site: http://www.fishwildlife.org
The Association of Fish and Wildlife Agencies promotes fish management and conservation.

Canadian Sportfishing Industry Association (CSIA)
1434 Chemong Road, Unit 11
Peterborough, ON K9J 6X2
Canada
(705) 745-8433
Web site: http://www.csia.ca
This organization works to preserve fishing opportunities for Canada's residents and visitors through education and management.

FishAmerica Foundation
225 Reinekers Lane, Suite 420
Alexandria, VA 22314
(703) 519-9691

Web site: http://www.fishamerica.org
The FishAmerica Foundation is the conservation and research foundation of the American Sportfishing Association. It focuses on keeping the nation's fish and waters healthy.

Fisheries and Oceans Canada
200 Kent Street, 13th Floor
Station 13E228
Ottawa, ON K1A 0E6
Canada
(613) 993-0999
Web site: http://www.dfo-mpo.gc.ca
This is Canada's official site for information on all fish-related topics in Canada. The site contains a lot of useful information.

Fresh Water Fishing Hall of Fame and Museum
P.O. Box 690
10360 Hall of Fame Drive
Hayward, WI 54843
(715) 634-4440
Web site: http://www.freshwaterfishing.org
This organization is the international headquarters for education and promotion of freshwater sport fishing.

National Wildlife Federation
P.O. Box 1583
Merrifield, VA 22116
(800) 822-9919
Web site: http://www.nwf.org

This organization works to protect and restore wildlife habitats across the United States.

Ontario Federation of Anglers and Hunters
P.O. Box 2800
Peterborough, ON K9J 8L5
Canada
(705) 748-6324
Web site: http://www.ofah.org
The organization promotes fish and wildlife conservation. It focuses on fish hatcheries and improving habitats.

Professional Anglers Association
P.O. Box 655
1102 Main Street
Benton, KY 42025
(270) 527-2030
Web site: http://fishpaa.com
The Professional Anglers Association provides education to anglers to increase interest in the sport and promote good conservation practices.

Recreational Boating & Fishing Foundation
500 Montgomery Street, Suite 300
Alexandria, VA 22314
(703) 519-0013
Web site: http//www.rbff.org
This organization works to increase participation in angling and boating and conserve, protect, and restore the nation's aquatic natural resources.

U.S. Environmental Protection Agency (EPA)
Ariel Rios Building
1200 Pennsylvania Avenue NW
Washington, DC 20460
(202) 272-0167
Web site: http://www.epa.gov
The Environmental Protection Agency is in charge of protecting people and the nation's air, water, and land.

U.S. Fish and Wildlife Service
1849 C Street NW
Washington, DC 20240
(800) 344-9453
Web site: http://www.fws.gov
This government agency conserves, protects, and enhances fish, wildlife, and plants and their habitats.

Web Sites

Due to the changing nature of Internet links, Rosen Publishing has developed an online list of Web sites related to the subject of this book. This site is updated regularly. Please use this link to access the list:

http://www.rosenlinks.com/FISH/Wall

For Further Reading

Bagur, Daniel. *Where the Fish Are: An Angler's Guide to Fish Behavior.* New York, NY: McGraw-Hill, 2009.

Beatty, Richard. *Rivers, Lakes, Streams, and Ponds.* Mankato, MN: Heinemann-Raintree, 2010.

Blaisdell, Harold. *Tricks That Take Fish: The Definitive Guide to Catching Freshwater Gamefish on Bait, Lures, and Flies*. New York, NY: Skyhorse Publishing, 2012.

Bourne, Wade. *Basic Fishing: A Beginner's Guide*. New York, NY: Skyhorse Publishing, 2011.

Bowen, Scott, and David Dirks. *Knack Fishing for Everyone: A Complete Illustrated Guide.* Gilbert, AZ: Knack, 2009.

Bramwell, Martyn. Planetwatch. New York, NY: Dorling Kindersley, 2009.

Capenter, Tom. *Freshwater Fishing: Bass, Trout, Walleye, Catfish, and More*. Minneapolis, MN: Lerner Publications, 2012.

Desonie, Dana. *Hydrosphere: Freshwater Systems and Pollution.* New York, NY: Chelsea House Publishers, 2008.

DK Publishing. *Let's Go Fishing.* New York, NY: DK Children, 2008.

Geiger, Beth. *Clean Water.* New York, NY: Flash Point, 2009.

Howard, Melanie. *Freshwater Fishing for Kids.* Mankato, MN: Capstone Press, 2012.

Jeffery, S. B. *A Beginner's Guide to the Freshwater Fish of the Great Lakes*. Baldwin City, KS: Webster's Digital Services, 2011.

Kaye, Cathryn Berger, and Philippe Cousteau. *Going Blue: A Teen Guide to Saving Our Oceans, Lakes, Rivers, and Wetlands.* Minneapolis, MN: Free Spirit Publishing, 2010.

Le Tutla, Matt. *Professional Fishing Tips and Techniques: The Ultimate Guide.* Seattle, WA: CreateSpace, 2010.

Mladenik, Mike. *Northwoods Walleye.* Seattle, WA: CreateSpace, 2011.

Olson, Douglas. *The Complete Fishing Book*. Raleigh, NC: Lulu.com, 2011.

Pappert, Edward. *Do You Want to Catch a Fish?* North Charleston, SC:

BookSurge Publishing, 2010.
Rau, Dana Meachen. *Water Safety.* Salt Lake City, UT: Benchmark Books, 2009.
Scheibe, Nancy. *Willie Walleye Underwater Adventures.* Ely, MN: Singing River Publications, 2009.
Shellhaas, Dave D., and Steve A. Shellhaas. *Outdoor Kids Club Ultimate Fishing Guide*. Greenville, OH: Miami Valley Outdoor Media, 2011.
Silverstein, Alvin. *Global Warming.* Minneapolis, MN: Twenty-First Century Books, 2009.
Underwood, Lamar, ed. *1001 Fishing Tips: The Ultimate Guide to Finding and Catching More and Bigger Fish.* New York, NY: Skyhorse Publishing, 2010.
Webb, R. G. *Walleye, the Moving Target: Stories and Information for the Aspiring Angler.* Bloomington, IN: Xlibris, 2011.
Zarley, Craig. *Catching Canoe Country Walleyes: Quetico and Boundary Waters Jig Fishing Secrets.* Seattle, WA: CreateSpace, 2012.

BIBLIOGRAPHY

Baron, Frank. *What Fish Don't Want You to Know: An Insider's Guide to Freshwater Fishing.* Camden, ME: International Marine/Ragged Mountain Press, 2003.

Breining, Greg. *A Hard-Water World: Ice Fishing and Why We Do It.* St. Paul, MN: Minnesota Historical Society Press, 2008.

Cassell, Jay. *The Ultimate Guide to Fishing Skills, Tactics, and Techniques: A Comprehensive Guide to Catching Bass, Trout, Salmon, Walleyes, Panfish, Saltwater Gamefish, and Much More.* New York, NY: Skyhorse Publishing, 2012.

Freshwater Angler, eds. *The Complete Guide to Freshwater Fishing.* Minnetonka, MN: Creative Publishing, 2002.

Hoffman, Justin. "Walleye Fishing Tackle Guide." 2012. Retrieved September 3, 2012 (http://www.basspro.com/webapp/wcs/stores/servlet/CFPageC?storeId=10151&catalogID=10051&langId=-1).

In-Fisherman. "Walleye." 2012. Retrieved September 1, 2012 (http://www.in-fisherman.com/walleye).

Inman, Ed, Lenox Dick, and Gordon Steinmetz. *Walleye Fishing Simplified.* Portland, OR: Frank Amato Publications, 1999.

Martin, Mark. *Pro Tactics: Walleye: Use the Secrets of the Pros to Catch More and Bigger Walleye.* Guilford, CT: Lyons Press, 2008.

Minnesota Department of Natural Resources. "How to Fish." 2012. Retrieved September 2, 2012 (http://www.dnr.state.mn.us/fishing/downtown/how.html).

Minnesota Department of Natural Resources. "Walleye." 2012. Retrieved September 12, 2012 (http://www.dnr.state.mn.us/fish/walleye/index.html).

National Oceanic and Atmospheric Administration. "NOAA Scientist, Doug Helton, Answers Kids' Questions on Gulf Oil Spill." 2012. Retrieved October 1, 2012 (http://www.education.noaa.gov/Ocean_and_Coasts/Oil_Spill_Doug_Helton.html).

Peterson, David H. (Naturalist, Two Harbors, MN) in discussion with the author, September 2012.

Quinn, Steve. "The World of Walleyes." 2012. Retrieved September 30, 2012 (http://www.in-fisherman.com/2012/08/23/the-world-of-walleyes).

Romanack, Mark. *Catch More Walleye*. Iola, WI: Krause Publications, 2000.

Schara, Ron. *Ron Schara's Minnesota Fishing Guide*. Golden Valley, MN: Tristan Outdoors, 2003.

Stange, Doug. *Walleye Location: Finding Walleyes in Lakes, Rivers, and Reservoirs: Expert Advice from North America's Leading Authority on Freshwater.* Baxter, MN: In-Fisherman, 1999.

U.S. Environmental Protection Agency. "Fish Consumption Advisories." April 27, 2012. Retrieved September 13, 2012 (http://water.epa.gov/scitech/swguidance/fishshellfish/fishadvisories).

U.S. Environmental Protection Agency. "Water: Pollution Prevention & Control." June 18, 2012. Retrieved September 18, 2012 (http://water.epa.gov/polwaste).

Walleye Hunter. "Walleye Fishing Articles Online." 2011. Retrieved September 1, 2012 (http://www.walleyehunter.com/articles.html).

Warye, Russ. *Walleye! The Top Ten Lakes and Rivers of North America.* Rhinelander, WI: Fishing Hot Spots, 2001.

INDEX

About the Author

Judy Monroe Peterson is a former health care, technical, and academic librarian and college faculty member; a biologist and research scientist; and curriculum editor with more than thirty years of experience. She is a writer and editor of K–12 and post-high school curriculum materials on a variety of subjects, including biology, life science, and the environment. She enjoys fishing for walleye with her family on the lakes of Minnesota.

About the Consultant

Benjamin Cowan has more than twenty years of both freshwater and saltwater angling experience. In addition to being an avid outdoorsman, Cowan is a member of many conservation organizations. He currently resides in west Tennessee.

Photo Credits

Cover, pp. 1, 3, 7, 12, 16, 19, 22, 25, 28, 34, 41, 43, 50 Tyler Olson/Shutterstock.com; pp. 4–5, 7, 12, 16, 19, 22, 25, 28, 34, 41, 43, 50 (water) © iStockphoto.com/MichaelJay; p. 5 © James Smedley/Design Pics Inc./Getty Images; p. 8 Kansas City Star/McClatchy-Tribune/Getty Images; pp. 10–11, 17, 23, 30–31, 35, 39 © AP Images; p. 14 © iStockphoto.com/Jim Jurica; p. 21 © iStockphoto.com/Steve Brigman; p. 26 NOAA, Great Lakes Environmental Research Laboratory; p. 32 Sam Cook/MCT/Landov; pp. 36–37 Dennis Anderson/MCT/Landov; p. 44 © Minneapolis Star Tribune/ZUMA Press; p. 47 AFP/Getty Images; p. 49 Mike Greenlar/The Post-Standard/Landov; back cover and interior silhouettes (figures) © iStockphoto.com/A-Digit, Hemera/Thinkstock; back cover and interior silhouette (grass) © iStockphoto.com/Makhnach_M; back cover silhouette (hook) iStockphoto.com/Jason Derry.

Designer: Nicole Russo; Editor: Kathy Kuhtz Campbell;
Photo Researcher: Amy Feinberg